D0376249

CAPTAIN FACT
EGYPTIAN
ADVENTURE

Captain Fact Space Adventure
Captain Fact Dinosaur Adventure
Captain Fact Creepy-Crawly Adventure
Captain Fact Egyptian Adventure

Captain Fact Egyptian Adventure

by

Knife & Packer

Hyperion Books for Children
New York

First published in the United Kingdom by Egmont Books Limited, London

Printed in the United States of America
First U.S. edition, 2005
1 3 5 7 9 10 8 6 4 2

This book is set in 13/19 Excelsior.

ISBN 0-7868-5574-6

Visit www.hyperionbooksforchildren.com

CONTENTS

STARR
CLIFF THORNHILL
TV'S WORST WEATHERMAN
PUDDLES
THE ONLY
WEATHERDOG ON TV
CAPTAIN FACT
THE WORLD'S FIRST
INFORMATION SUPERHERO
KNOWLEDGE
CAPTAIN FACT'S
FAITHFUL SIDEKICK

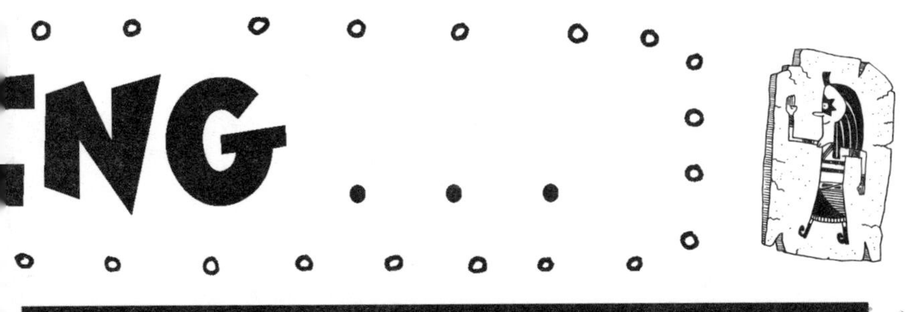
NG . . .

LUCY
HEAD OF MAKEUP AND CLIFF'S BEST FRIEND
THE BOSS
HE'S SCARY!
PROFESSOR MINUSCULE
HEAD OF THE FACT CAVE AND THE BRAINS BEHIND THE MISSIONS
FACTORELLA
PROFESSOR MINUSCULE'S DAUGHTER AND ALL-AROUND WHIZ KID
F

CHAPTER 1

ARCHAEOLOGIST IN DEEP . . .

TV's worst weatherman, Cliff Thornhill, and his copresenter, Puddles the dog, hadn't had a day off from work in forever. So they were excited to get out of the office and go to the City Museum.

"It's great that our day off is on the same day as the talk from the world's most famous archaeologist," said Cliff. "These are the hottest tickets in town! Sir Ramsbottom Tickell's just been to Egypt, and he's made some amazing discoveries."

But there was one thing spoiling their perfect day . . . the Boss had decided to come!

"What's the Boss doing here?" whispered Puddles. He had to keep his voice down when other people were around. They couldn't know he spoke—it would give away his identity.

"He must have seen the invitations on my desk," said Cliff. They took their seats in the auditorium and waited for Sir Ramsbottom.

"The Boss is always snooping," said Puddles. "Last week I'm sure he was sniffing around for my licorice–flavored dog biscuits."

Around them the crowd was beginning to get restless. There was no sign of the famous archaeologist.

That's strange, Cliff thought. Sir Ramsbottom's never late.

"Thornhill!" shouted the Boss. "What's going on? Where's this archaeologist of yours?"

"Well, um, I'm sure he'll be here any minute," stuttered Cliff. "He's probably just dusting a mummy and . . . uh . . . polishing up his speech."

Just then the doors of the auditorium burst open. It was Lucy, Cliff's friend from the Makeup department.

"What are you doing here?" screamed the Boss. "I don't remember giving *you* the day off!"

"Have you heard the news?" panted Lucy. "Sir Ramsbottom's missing! He is lost in the Great Pyramid!"

"Lost in a pyramid?" the Boss said. He was shocked.

"Yes! He discovered a secret passage into the Great Pyramid," said Lucy. "The only problem is that he hasn't been able to find his way back out. He's trapped in the pyramid, and no one can reach him."

"I smell a big story!" shouted the Boss. "Everyone, back to the office—NOW! That includes you, Thornhill, and your mutt. I've just canceled your day off!"

As they raced back to the office, Lucy filled Cliff and Puddles in on the rest of the story. "Rescue teams have tried everything, but they just can't seem to find him. Sir Ramsbottom is the only person alive who knew about the secret entrance!"

When they got back to the studio, Cliff and Puddles slipped off to their office.

That's strange, thought Lucy, watching them go. Sir Ramsbottom is Cliff's hero. I thought he'd be upset about his disappearance. How can he think about the weather at a time like this?

As soon as the office door shut, Cliff turned to Puddles.

"Well, do you know what this means, Puddles?" he asked.

"We've had our day off ruined by an archaeologist with a bad sense of direction," Puddles replied bitterly. "I told you we should have gone to the new canine theme park, Doggie Land. They've just opened the Bones of Fire ride."

"Don't be silly, Puddles," said Cliff. "That's not what this means. This is a mission for Captain Fact!" With that, he pulled a lever next to him to reveal the entrance to the Fact Cave. . . .

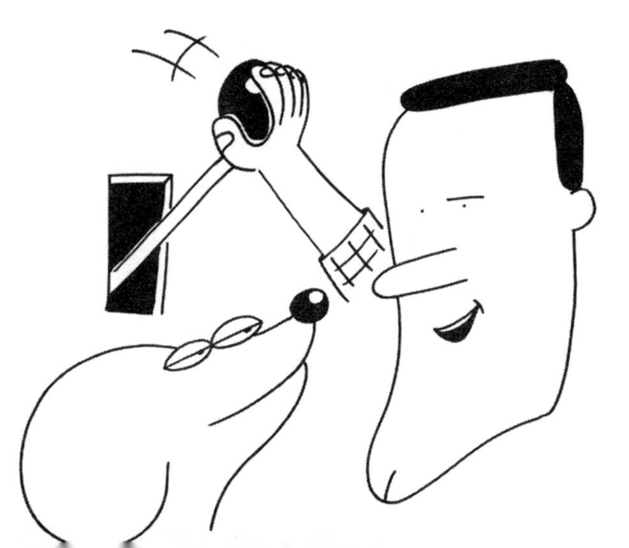

FACT CAVE

CAPTAIN FACT
KNOWLEDGE

"We've got to get to that pyramid as soon as possible," panted Captain Fact as they ran through the Fact Cave corridors. "Sir Ramsbottom will be running out of air."

"Why doesn't he just follow the exit signs inside the pyramid?" asked Knowledge. "Or use an elevator?"

"Exit signs? Elevators?" said Captain Fact. "The whole point of the pyramids was to keep people out and, if you did sneak in, to make sure you stayed in!"

And with that his mask began to wiggle as he felt the start of a . . .

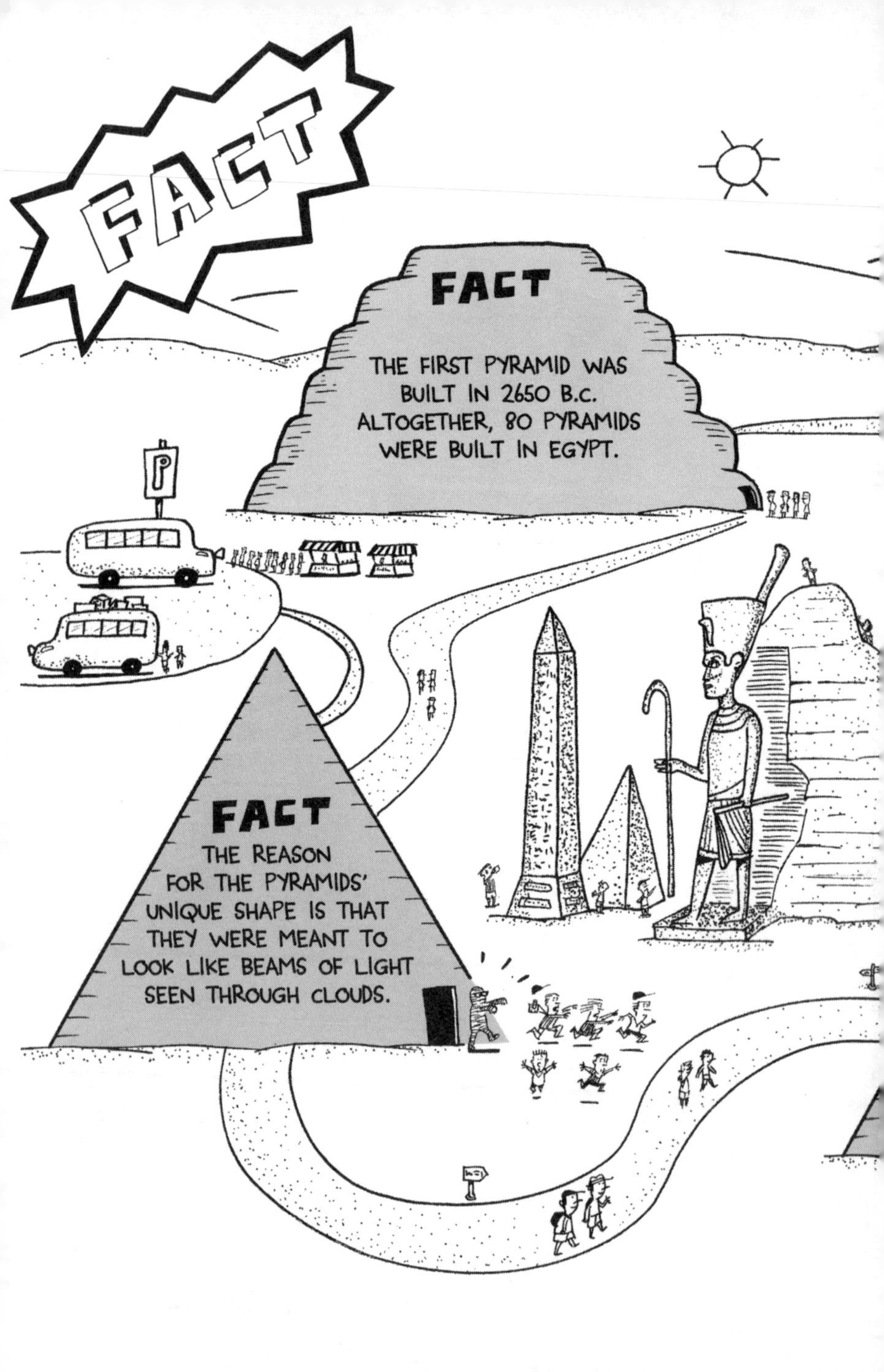
FACT
FACT
THE FIRST PYRAMID WAS BUILT IN 2650 B.C. ALTOGETHER, 80 PYRAMIDS WERE BUILT IN EGYPT.
P
FACT
THE REASON FOR THE PYRAMIDS' UNIQUE SHAPE IS THAT THEY WERE MEANT TO LOOK LIKE BEAMS OF LIGHT SEEN THROUGH CLOUDS.

FACT
PYRAMIDS ARE GIANT TOMBS. THEY WERE BUILT TO PROTECT THE BODIES OF THE RULERS OF ANCIENT EGYPT, THE PHARAOHS, WHO WERE BURIED DEEP INSIDE.
FACT
THE PYRAMIDS ARE GINORMOUS! THE GREAT PYRAMID OF CHEOPS IS MORE THAN 452 FEET TALL! THAT'S HIGHER THAN THE STATUE OF LIBERTY! IT'S MADE FROM OVER 2.3 MILLION BLOCKS OF STONE AND TOOK 20 YEARS TO BUILD!
FACT
PYRAMIDS ARE FULL OF SECRET PASSAGEWAYS AND FALSE DOORS. THESE WERE MEANT TO KEEP OUT GRAVE ROBBERS WHO MIGHT HAVE TRIED TO COME IN AND STEAL THE PHARAOHS' TREASURES!
ATTACK!!!

"Yikes!" said Knowledge. "That sounds scary. You'll never get *me* in a pyramid!"

Just then, the Nerve Center doors slid open.

STEP BACK IN TIME

"At last! Captain Fact and Knowledge," said Professor Minuscule, the world's shortest genius. "If you'd taken much longer I would have been mummified!" He looked at his watch. "There's no time to waste; we have an archaeologist to save!"

"As long as we don't have to go inside a pyramid," said Knowledge nervously. He was still thinking about the fact attack.

"That's not what we have to worry about right now. First we have to get you back to the time of the ancient Egyptians," said Professor Minuscule.

"Back in time?" gulped Captain Fact. "Not again!"

"I'm afraid so," said Professor Minuscule. "No one has been down this secret passage and come out alive since the pyramid was built. The *only* way to save Sir Ramsbottom is to send you back to ancient Egypt. I've been tinkering with time travel since your last adventure and I've come up with a brand-new time-traveling concept."

Professor Minuscule walked over to his control panel and pressed a

button. Suddenly, there was a high-pitched wobbling noise, and then a virtual doorway materialized before them.

"Gentlemen, and dog, I give you . . . the Time Portal!" said Professor Minuscule. "Step through this, and you literally step into the past."

"Step into the past!" exclaimed Captain Fact. "How can we do that?"

"It's actually quite simple. The Time Portal liquefies every molecule in your body, then sends them all back in time before putting them back together in the designated time period," said Professor Minuscule. "Your designated time period is ancient Egypt, 2589 B.C."

As Captain Fact and Knowledge nervously contemplated stepping back 4,500 years, Professor Minuscule's daughter, Factorella, suddenly dropped in through the ceiling. She slid down a long pole.

"When are we going, Dad? I can't wait to get into that pyramid," gushed Factorella when she landed on the ground. "The curse of the mummy doesn't scare me!"

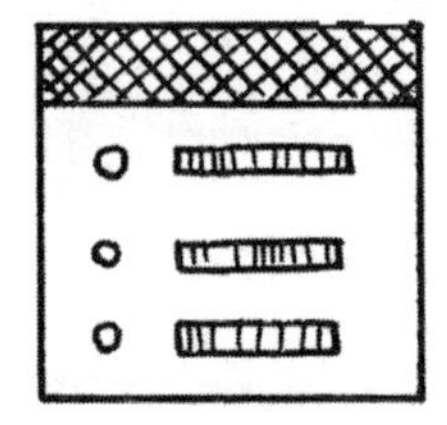

"Curse of the mummy?" said Knowledge, quaking. "No one said anything about a curse."

"**KER-FACT!**" piped up Captain Fact. "When Tutankhamen's tomb was opened in 1923, several people involved in the excavation died under mysterious circumstances."

"We don't have time for facts," interrupted Professor Minuscule. "And, Factorella, you know you're too young to go on missions. I told you to research Egypt on Factotum, the Fact Cave's supercomputer. Did you find anything interesting?"

"Loads! Check it out," Factorella replied.

THE ANCIENT EGYPTIANS WERE AROUND FOR MORE THAN 3,000 YEARS, FROM 3100 B.C. UNTIL EGYPT BECAME PART OF THE ROMAN EMPIRE IN 30 B.C. THERE WERE THREE MAIN PERIODS DURING THESE TIMES:
OLD KINGDOM: 2686 B.C.–2181 B.C. THE PYRAMIDS AND THE SPHINX WERE BUILT.

MIDDLE KINGDOM:
2055 B.C.–1650 B.C.
AFTER A PERIOD OF WAR, THE PHARAOH MONTUHOTEP REUNITED UPPER AND LOWER EGYPT.
NEW KINGDOM:
1550 B.C.–1069 B.C.
DURING THIS PERIOD THE TEMPLE OF LUXOR AND THE VALLEY OF THE KINGS WERE BUILT. TUTANKHAMEN RULED.

"Thanks, Factorella. That was important information. Now, don't you have some homework to do?" asked Professor Minuscule. Turning to Captain Fact and Knowlege, he added,"I've got to set the Time Portal to 2589 B.C."

As Professor Minuscule fiddled with the Time Portal, Factorella slyly walked up to Captain Fact.

"Psst! This might help you," she said. She slipped him a rolled-up piece of paper.

"Factorella, I thought I told you to go to your room," Professor Minuscule said in a tired voice. "Any more nonsense from you and you're grounded!"

As Factorella moped, Captain Fact unrolled the piece of paper she had given him.

It was a hand-drawn map of Egypt. . . .

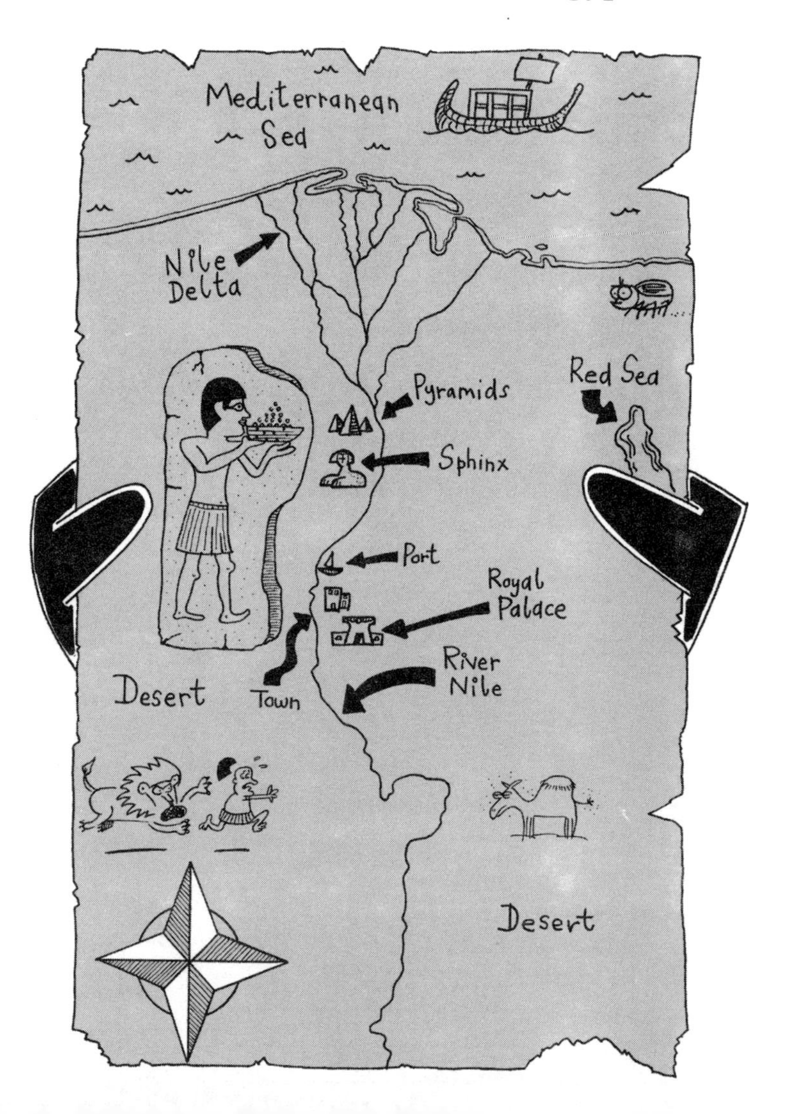

"All right! The Time Portal is now set to take you to ancient Egypt," declared Professor Minuscule. "Let's just hope you don't step into something nasty, like a battle or a plague."

"A plague?" whimpered Knowledge. This mission kept getting scarier and scarier. But there was no turning back now.

"Good luck, gentlemen," said Professor Minuscule, "and prepare to say, 'Hello, Pharaoh!'"

Without another word, Captain Fact and Knowledge stepped through the Time Portal and into the unknown.

SECRET FACT!

(SHHH! DON'T TELL!)
SO HOW DO WE KNOW THAT FACTORELLA WILL GROW UP TO BE A SUPERHERO?

EVEN AS A BABY, FACTORELLA STOOD OUT FROM THE CROWD!

GOO-GOO!

GA-GA!

CONSTELLATION!

WHILE HER FRIENDS WERE STILL LEARNING TO WALK, SHE COULD ALREADY JUGGLE, BREATHE FIRE, AND DO THE TRAPEZE—ALL AT THE SAME TIME!

AND A FEW YEARS LATER, WHILE THE OTHER KIDS WERE OUTSIDE RIDING THEIR BIKES, FACTORELLA WAS INDOORS, TURBOCHARGING HERS. . . .

NOW THAT FACTORELLA'S IN SCHOOL, IT'S EVEN MORE OBVIOUS THAT SHE'S NOT LIKE THE OTHER CHILDREN. . . .

SHE'S EVEN BEEN BANNED FROM PARTICIPATING IN SCHOOL SPORTS DAY. . . . SHE'S WON TOO MANY MEDALS!

SO IT DOESN'T TAKE A GENIUS TO SEE THAT FACTORELLA WILL GROW UP TO BE A SUPERHERO. BUT IN THE MEANTIME . . .

CHAPTER 3

HELLO, PHARAOH!

As Captain Fact and Knowledge emerged in ancient Egypt, the Time Portal fizzled and then faded away.

What they saw when they looked around was shocking. All around them were towering columns, colossal granite statues, and thrones inlaid with precious stones.

"That felt weird," said Knowledge. He was still recovering from the time-traveling. "It was like gargling a giant soda and having my toes tickled by a thousand ants, at the same time."

"Shhh, Knowledge," whispered Captain Fact. He looked worried. "It appears we're in some sort of royal palace. And look, that must be the pharaoh!"

"Why are all those people on their hands and knees?" asked Knowledge. "Did the pharaoh lose his contact lens?"

"Don't be silly, Knowledge," said Captain Fact. "**KER-FACT!** The pharaoh's subjects were supposed to kiss the ground before him as a mark of respect. We must have stumbled into some sort of special occasion."

"Special occasion?" Knowledge repeated cheerfully. "Great! Do you think

there will be dancing? Or Pin-the-Tail-on-the-Donkey? I love special occasions."

"I don't think we've been invited to *this* special occasion," said Captain Fact. "Plus, we've got a pyramid puzzle to solve. And we can't do that if we stay here—this place is crawling with guards! Let's go."

Captain Fact and Knowledge tried and tried to find a way out of the palace. They ran through corridors, down stairs, past arches, and around columns. There were people everywhere!
"The pharaoh must be very popular," said Knowledge. "*We've* never had this many friends over."
"They're not friends," Captain Fact replied. "**KER-FACT!** The pharoah's palace is more like a headquarters than a home. All of these people help run Egypt."

The superheroes suddenly found themselves in the royal kitchen.

"I'm starting to like ancient Egypt," Knowlege said. All around them were tables groaning with the finest Egyptian foods: dates, figs, cucumbers, melons, pomegranates, grapes, and large jars of honey.

"There's no time for eating, Knowledge!" Captain Fact said. "We're going to hide in these empty jars and wait for a while."

Very carefully, Captain Fact and Knowledge slipped inside the two decorated jars. "I'd love to have been a pharaoh," whispered Knowledge. "People worshipping me, loads of great food . . ."

"Don't forget all the fabulous gifts from visitors to the court," said Captain Fact, as his head began to throb and he got ready for a . . .

FACT
FACT
PHARAOHS HAD TO
LEAD THE ARMY INTO BATTLE,
CONTROL EGYPT'S WEALTH, JUDGE
CRIMINALS . . . AND WERE BELIEVED
TO BE LIVING GODS, TOO!
FACT
YOU COULD BECOME
PHARAOH AT ANY
AGE. THE PHARAOH
PEPY II BECAME
PHARAOH AT THE
AGE OF SIX AND
RULED FOR 94 YEARS!
FACT
ONE OF THE MOST FAMOUS
PHARAOHS WAS A WOMAN NAMED
CLEOPATRA. ALL PHARAOHS,
INCLUDING FEMALE PHARAOHS,
HAD TO WEAR FALSE
BEARDS AT CEREMONIES.

FACT
THE PHARAOH'S OLDEST CHILD WOULD GO THROUGH LOTS OF TRAINING BEFORE BECOMING THE NEXT PHARAOH. HE WOULD LEARN HOW TO BE A LEADER AS WELL AS AN EXPERT HUNTER.
FACT
PHARAOH LITERALLY MEANS "GREAT HOUSE," BECAUSE PHARAOHS LIVED IN A HUGE ROYAL PALACE.
ATTACK!!!

All of a sudden, Captain Fact and Knowledge felt themselves being lifted up. . . .

"What's going on?" whispered Knowledge.

"Well, I'm hoping my plan's working and we are now being carried out of the palace," said Captain Fact. He was right. A pair of burly Egyptians had hoisted the jars containing our two superheroes onto their shoulders and were carrying them out into the town.

CHAPTER 4

WALK LIKE AN EGYPTIAN

Eventually the jars containing Captain Fact and Knowledge were dumped in the backyard of a local shop.

"We did it! We got out of the palace!" cried Captain Fact, brushing off his cape. "Now we just have to find a boat."

"A boat?" asked Knowledge. "I thought we were surrounded by desert."

"We are," said Captain Fact matter-of-factly, "but the best way to get around Egypt is on the River Nile. We've got to get to the Great Pyramid soon. We've got an archaeologist to save!"

Just then the owner of the shop appeared. The last thing he had been expecting to see was a superhero and a talking dog.

He shouted angrily at them and started chasing after them with a broom.

"I don't think the locals want to meet us," said Captain Fact. "Let's get out of here." With that, they took off.

When they finally stopped running, they found themselves on a busy street. Captain Fact and Knowledge quickly realized that everyone was staring at them.

"We're going to need a disguise," Captain Fact said under his breath. "Let's get off the main road."

They took the first turn off the main street and found themselves in a dusty, deserted back alley.

“We hit the jackpot,” Captain Fact exclaimed when he saw a clothesline full of clothes. “Time to go native!”

“I’ve always wanted to wear a kilt!” said Knowledge as he sized up a pair of Egyptian knickers.

"That's not a kilt, Knowledge! But we'll still need to leave some sort of payment," said Captain Fact. He was slipping into a linen loincloth. "Have you got any dog biscuits?" he asked.

"Only a couple of bags," whined Knowledge. "Can't you leave the Fact Watch instead?"

"The Fact Watch? You know I can't leave that," said Captain Fact. "It's our only contact with home."

Knowledge sighed and reluctantly handed over a bag of butterscotch-flavored doggie snacks.

With their superhero outfits safely hidden under Captain Fact's headdress, they were able to walk unnoticed among the locals.

"Time to use that map Factorella gave us," said Captain Fact. "Now, Knowledge, if I'm not badly mistaken, the Nile is due west of us."

As they made their way toward the Nile, they were amazed by the bustling, humming streets around them.

"Ancient Egypt was one of the great civilizations of the world," said Captain Fact, as his ears began to wobble and he launched into another . . .

FACT ATTACK!!!
FACT
ANCIENT EGYPTIAN HOUSES HAD VERY LITTLE FURNITURE: JUST A CHEST FOR STORAGE AND A COUPLE OF STOOLS. EVEN THE COOKING WAS DONE ON THE FLOOR.
FACT
EGYPTIAN HOUSES WERE CONSTRUCTED OF BRICKS MADE FROM MUD FROM THE NILE. THE KITCHEN WAS ALWAYS BUILT FAR AWAY FROM THE LIVING QUARTERS BECAUSE OF THE STINKY COOKING SMELLS!

FACT
IN THE SUMMERTIME IT WOULD GET SO HOT THAT PEOPLE WOULD SLEEP UP ON THE ROOF!
FACT
WHILE THE PHARAOH SLEPT IN A BED, MOST EGYPTIANS HAD TO SLEEP ON EITHER A BARE MATTRESS STUFFED WITH STRAW OR WOOL, A MAT, OR JUST THE BARE FLOOR.
FACT
WEALTHY HOUSES HAD LIMESTONE TOILETS. BUT MOST ANCIENT EGYPTIANS HAD TO MAKE DO WITH A WOODEN "TOILET STOOL." UNDER THE SEAT WOULD BE A CERAMIC BOWL TO CATCH . . . YOU KNOW WHAT.

Suddenly, there it was—the Nile, just where Factorella had shown it to be on the map.

"Check it out, Knowledge," said Captain Fact. "It's ancient Egypt's highway. A multi-laned road that joins north and south!"

CHAPTER 5

NILE BE BACK

"Well, Knowledge," said Captain Fact after he had stopped staring at the busy river. He couldn't believe his eyes. "The pyramids should be downstream from here. We're going to have to get onto a boat."

"I think I saw the perfect one for us," said Knowledge. He pointed at a lavish, golden vessel. "Check it out; they've got music, food, dancers. . . ."

"**KER-FACT!** Ancient Egyptians were the first people to have tourism," said Captain Fact. "The wealthy citizens used to take pleasure cruises up the Nile!"

"Dinner and dancing . . . I can't wait," said Knowledge. He started to walk toward the luxurious boat.

"Stop right there, Knowledge," Captain Fact ordered. "We're supposed to be undercover. We need to sneak onto a boat and hide until we get to the Great Pyramid. And *I* have just the one!"

Knowledge looked where Captain Fact was pointing. He groaned. A herd of cows were being led up a wobbly gangplank and onto the deck of a battered old cattle barge. Swarms of flies buzzed around, and the air was heavy with the smell of cow manure.

"Grab a cow and hold on tight!" said Captain Fact. "Here we go again!"

Once on board, Captain Fact and Knowledge found themselves penned in with dozens of mooing cows.

"I'm up to my knees in cow," moaned Knowledge.

"Don't worry, Knowledge, we should be there in no time," said Captain Fact. The boat creaked into action.

"I hope so," said Knowledge. "If I get another hoof on my paw . . ."

"The Nile's amazing, Knowledge," said Captain Fact, cutting off his sidekick's whining. "Did you know it's the longest river in the world? Without it there would not have been an ancient Egypt."

And with that his toes began to tingle, and he felt the start of a .

FACT
FACT
EVERY YEAR
THE NILE FLOODED,
AND THE SILT
DEPOSITED ON THE
BANKS MADE THE
LAND PERFECT FOR
GROWING CROPS.
FACT
THE NILE
HAS ALWAYS
BEEN FULL OF
CROCODILES. IN
ANCIENT EGYPT, TAME
CROCS WERE POPULAR
PETS—THEY WERE FED
FINE FOODS AND DRESSED
IN JEWELRY!

ATTACK!!!
FACT
THE NILE WAS SO IMPORTANT TO THE ANCIENT EGYPTIANS IT EVEN HAD ITS OWN SET OF GODS. SOME OF THESE NILE GODS WERE SYMBOLS OF FERTILITY.
FACT
OVER 90% OF EGYPT IS DESERT, SO MOST ANCIENT EGYPTIANS LIVED BY THE NILE AND THE CANALS RUNNING OFF IT.
FACT
THE PHARAOH TRAVELED THE NILE IN A MAGNIFICENT BOAT THAT WAS BURIED WITH HIM FOR HIS USE IN THE AFTERLIFE.

When the boat finally docked, Captain Fact and Knowledge were glad to find themselves back on dry land.

"I thought we'd be closer to the pyramids by now," said Knowledge as he squinted at the horizon.

"So did I. According to the map they should be straight ahead," said Captain Fact. "Looks like we'd better start walking."

Captain Fact and Knowledge set out on the final part of their journey across the desert to the pyramids. Suddenly there was a thunderous rumbling, and the ground began to shake.

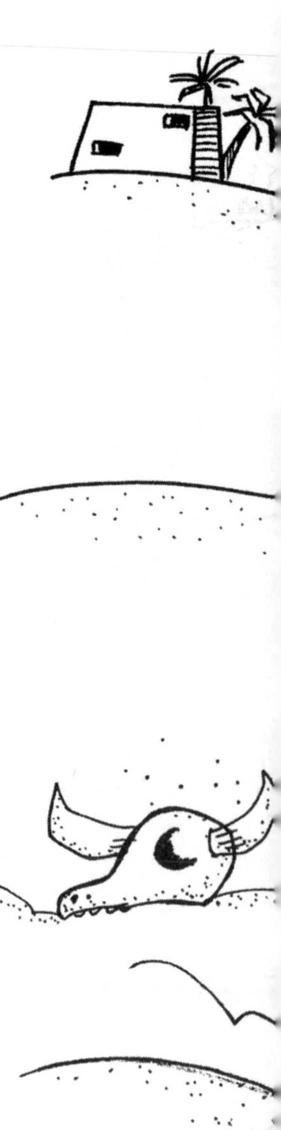

As the rumbling got louder and louder, a black cloud of dust gathered on the horizon. Knowledge started to panic. . . .

"What's that noise?" he asked. "Is it an earthquake? Is it an avalanche? Did the pyramid collapse?"

"None of the above, Knowledge," Captain Fact replied calmly. "We appear to have stumbled into the middle of a battlefield. **KER-FACT!** The ancient Egyptians had to protect their borders from all kinds of nasty neighbors, including Hittites, Assyrians, and Nubians."

“Why are they coming at us? We haven’t done anything to them,” said Knowledge nervously.

“No, but we are standing right where two armies are about to fight,” said Captain Fact. “In a desert, there’s nowhere to hide. We are stuck! We need help!” With that, he activated the panic button on his Fact Watch.

Then Captain Fact and Knowledge braced themselves for impact. The two armies thundered toward each other.

Just before Captain Fact and Knowlege got trampled, Factorella appeared! She was hovering in the air above them in what looked like a miniature helicopter.

"Grab on to the rope!" she shouted. Once they were attached, Captain Fact and Knowledge were whisked into the air.

"What do you think of the TimeCopter? Pretty cool, huh?" asked Factorella as they flew away from the battle.

"It's fantastic," said Captain Fact. "Can we have one?"

"Not now," said Factorella. "This is just a prototype. Dad only let me use it because it was an emergency."

Factorella landed the TimeCopter by a herd of camels.

"Catch a camel and head north," she said. "That should bring you to the pyramids. I'd love to stay, but I've got to get back and do laundry."

"Thanks, Factorella," said Captain Fact. With a loud bang, the TimeCopter disappeared. Captain Fact and Knowledge grabbed a camel and set off.

CHAPTER 6
SPHINX JINX

With their camel charging along at top speed, it wasn't long before the pyramids were within reach.

"We're almost there, Knowledge," said Captain Fact as he surveyed the fast-approaching monuments.

"Look, there's a welcoming committee to meet us!" said Knowledge. He pointed to a large group of sweating Egyptian builders that had just come into view.

“I don’t think that’s a welcoming committee,” said Captain Fact, bringing the camel to a halt. There was a frenzy of activity all around them.

Captain Fact and Knowledge dismounted, and immediately, chisels and wooden mallets were put into their hands. They were pointed in the direction of a giant sculpture.

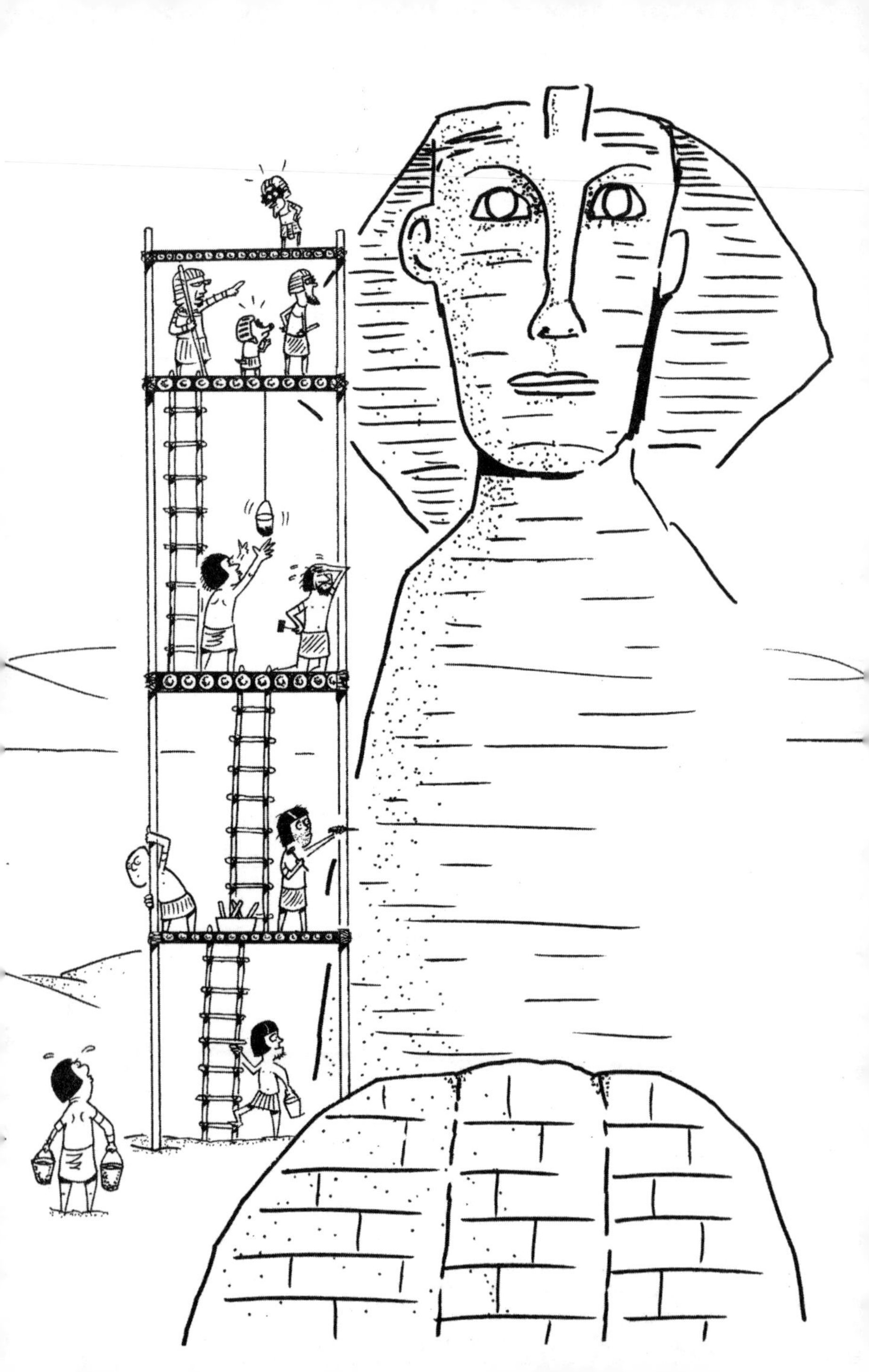

“They must think we’re builders,” whispered Captain Fact as they were taken up a very tall ladder. Then the other workers began chipping away at the giant rock face.

“But what are they building?” asked Knowledge. “It seems to be some sort of ginormous cat wearing a wig! Gross!”

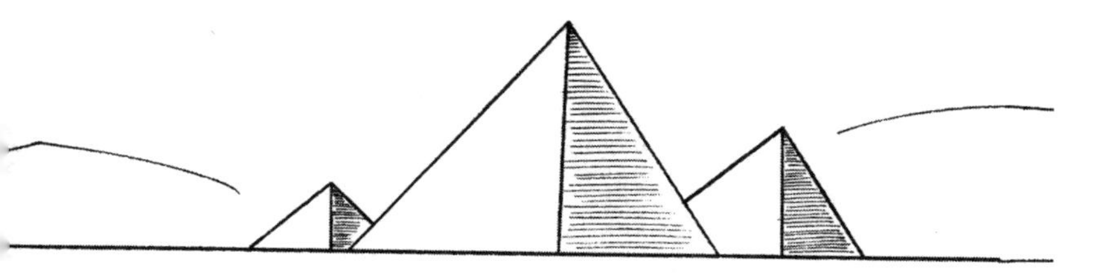

“It’s not a cat, Knowledge,” replied Captain Fact. “It’s the Sphinx of Giza.” And with that his elbow began to itch, and he felt the beginning of another . . .

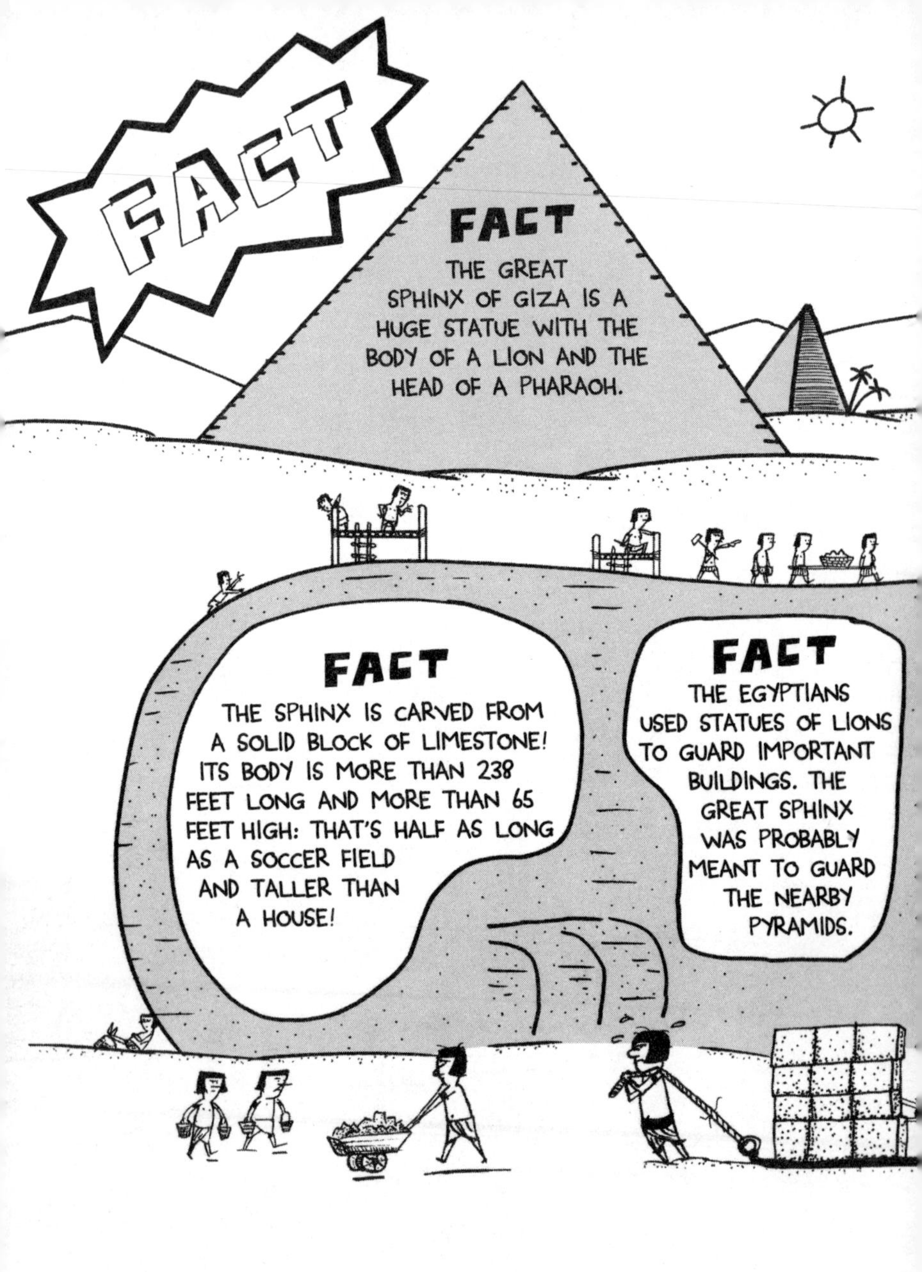
FACT
FACT
THE GREAT SPHINX OF GIZA IS A HUGE STATUE WITH THE BODY OF A LION AND THE HEAD OF A PHARAOH.
FACT
THE SPHINX IS CARVED FROM A SOLID BLOCK OF LIMESTONE! ITS BODY IS MORE THAN 238 FEET LONG AND MORE THAN 65 FEET HIGH: THAT'S HALF AS LONG AS A SOCCER FIELD AND TALLER THAN A HOUSE!
FACT
THE EGYPTIANS USED STATUES OF LIONS TO GUARD IMPORTANT BUILDINGS. THE GREAT SPHINX WAS PROBABLY MEANT TO GUARD THE NEARBY PYRAMIDS.

FACT
FOR LONG PERIODS OF ITS HISTORY THE SPHINX HAS BEEN BURIED UP TO ITS NECK IN SAND.
FACT
POLLUTION FROM MODERN CAIRO IS MAKING THE SPHINX START TO CRUMBLE. SOME PEOPLE BELIEVE THE BEST WAY TO PRESERVE THE GREAT STATUE MAY BE TO REBURY IT!
ATTACK!!!

From high up in the air Captain Fact and Knowledge heard a bell ringing. All around them the workers put down their tools.

"This must be some sort of Egyptian work break," whispered Captain Fact.

He and Knowledge joined the builders, who were snacking on honey cakes and figs.

"I don't think being a worker in ancient Egypt is so bad," said Knowledge. He was already happily munching his way through his fifteenth fig.

"Don't get too full, Knowledge, we've still got an archaeologist to save," said Captain Fact. Just then the bell sounded again, signaling the end of the break.

As the workmen returned to their posts, Captain Fact saw their opportunity.

"Quick, Knowledge, jump on that," said Captain Fact, pointing to something that looked like a boat—on sand. "This is our ticket out of here." Captain Fact and Knowledge perched on the pile of rubble, and it slowly began to lurch forward.

"We're being pulled way from the building site toward a dump," said Captain Fact. "We can hop off when we pass the pyramids."

"Okay, Knowledge, NOW!" said Captain Fact a few minutes later. They jumped and landed with a thud in the sand.

"I don't get it—there's three pyramids!" said Knowledge, dusting himself down.

"That's correct, Knowledge," said Captain Fact. "**KER-FACT!** There's the Pyramid of Mycerinus, the Pyramid of Chephren, and the one we want: the Great Pyramid of Cheops. That is the biggest of the three."

"Great," said Knowledge. "So we can just go in, find the secret tunnel, and be home in time for dinner."

"It's not going to be that easy," said Captain Fact. "Pyramids don't have front doors. We are going to have to be very clever."

CHAPTER 7
WRAP STARS

Captain Fact took a deep breath. "Mummies get carried in by the high priests," he said slowly. "So that means that if we get mummified, they'll carry *us* right in!" Then he added, "To the embalming hall!"

"Embalming hall?" whispered Knowledge.

"Yes. It's right next to the Pyramid of Cheops," said Captain Fact. "It's where the mummification takes place."

Ducking past guards, Captain Fact and Knowledge slipped into the embalming hall.

"We're in luck! It looks like they're preparing to mummify someone," said Captain Fact once they were inside. All around them knives were being sharpened and ointments were being mixed.

“Why is one of those people wearing a costume?” Knowledge asked nervously.

“Because he’s the high priest,” replied Captain Fact. “That mask depicts Anubis, one of the gods of the ancient Egyptians.” And with that his nose began to twitch, and he got ready for another . . .

FACT
FACT
ANUBIS: GOD OF EMBALMING. HE HAD A HUMAN BODY WITH THE HEAD OF A JACKAL.
FACT
THOTH: GOD OF WRITING, WISDOM, AND TIME. HE HAD THE HEAD OF AN IBIS.
THE ANCIENT EGYPTIANS WORSHIPPED HUNDREDS OF DIFFERENT GODS AND GODDESSES. HERE ARE JUST A FEW OF THE MOST IMPORTANT ONES. . . .

ATTACK!!!
FACT
RA: THE SUN GOD AND THE MOST SIGNIFICANT OF THE ANCIENT EGYPTIAN GODS. HE HAD THE HEAD OF A FALCON AND A HEADDRESS FEATURING A SUN DISK.
FACT
TAUERET: GODDESS OF FERTILITY, BIRTH, AND VENGEANCE. SHE HAD THE HEAD OF A HIPPOPOTAMUS AND THE BACK OF A CROCODILE.

A hush descended on the room as a body was carried in and placed on the marble embalming table.

"I think this is about to get gory," said Captain Fact with a shudder.

"What are they sticking up his nose?" asked Knowledge.

"That's a brain hook," replied Captain Fact. "It's inserted up the nose to scoop out the brain." Knowledge turned a light shade of green.

Next, the high priest held up a golden knife.

"What's he going to do with that?" whimpered Knowledge.

"Oh, don't worry, he's not chopping anything off," said Captain Fact, "he's going to make a cut on the side of the body to remove its internal organs!"

The high priest then brought out a bottle of wine.

"After all that, I'm not surprised he wants a glass of wine," Knowledge said with a sigh.

"He's not going to drink it," said Captain Fact. "Wine is used to rinse out the body. Then the body is covered in a salt called natron to preserve it. After all that, it is wrapped up in bandages."

The high priest completed the mummifying procedure, and the newly mummified body was held up. With great ceremony it was placed into a sparkling gold sarcophagus, and the lid was sealed shut.

As Knowledge slumped into a queasy heap on the floor, Captain Fact's eyes began to glow, and he got lost in a . . .

FACT
ANCIENT EGYPTIANS MUMMIFIED THE DEAD SO THAT THEIR BODIES WOULD BE PRESERVED FOR THE AFTERLIFE.
FACT
THE MUMMIFICATION PROCESS TOOK 70 DAYS, INCLUDING 40 DAYS TO DRY OUT THE BODY.
FACT
THE HEART WAS LEFT IN THE MUMMY BECAUSE IT WAS THOUGHT TO BE NEEDED FOR JUDGMENT IN THE NEXT WORLD.
FACT
THE LIVER, INTESTINES, LUNGS, EYEBALLS, AND STOMACH WERE PLACED IN JARS AND WERE STORED IN THE TOMB.

FACT
HUNDREDS OF FEET OF LINEN WERE USED FOR WRAPPING UP A MUMMY. LUCKY AMULETS AND JEWELRY WERE PLACED BETWEEN LAYERS OF FABRIC.
FACT
ONCE A BODY HAD BEEN MUMMIFIED, IT WAS PLACED IN A SARCOPHAGUS— A GIANT COFFIN MADE FROM STONE OR GOLD.
ATTACK!!!!

As the high priest and his assistants filed out of the hall, Captain Fact took action. Grabbing two bandages, he started winding them around Knowledge's paws.

"What are you doing?" asked Knowledge. "I don't need a Band-Aid!"

"It's not for a cut," said Captain Fact. "We're getting mummified."

CHAPTER 8

BURIED ALIVE!

Captain Fact and Knowledge carefully placed themselves among the glittering funeral items.

"Listen, Knowledge," whispered Captain Fact. "Here's the plan. The priests are going to bury their mummy in the pyramid's secret chamber. Because we are dressed like this, they're going to bury us, too! We'll be taken to the same chamber where Sir Ramsbottom is trapped, 4,500 years in the future! Hand over that last bag of doggie biscuits."

Before Knowledge could protest, the duo was picked up and carried off.

Captain Fact started to sprinkle dog biscuits behind them.

"What are you doing with my snacks?" asked Knowledge. "How can you be so disrespectful? They're pineapple-chunk flavor!"

"I'm leaving a trail," replied Captain Fact.

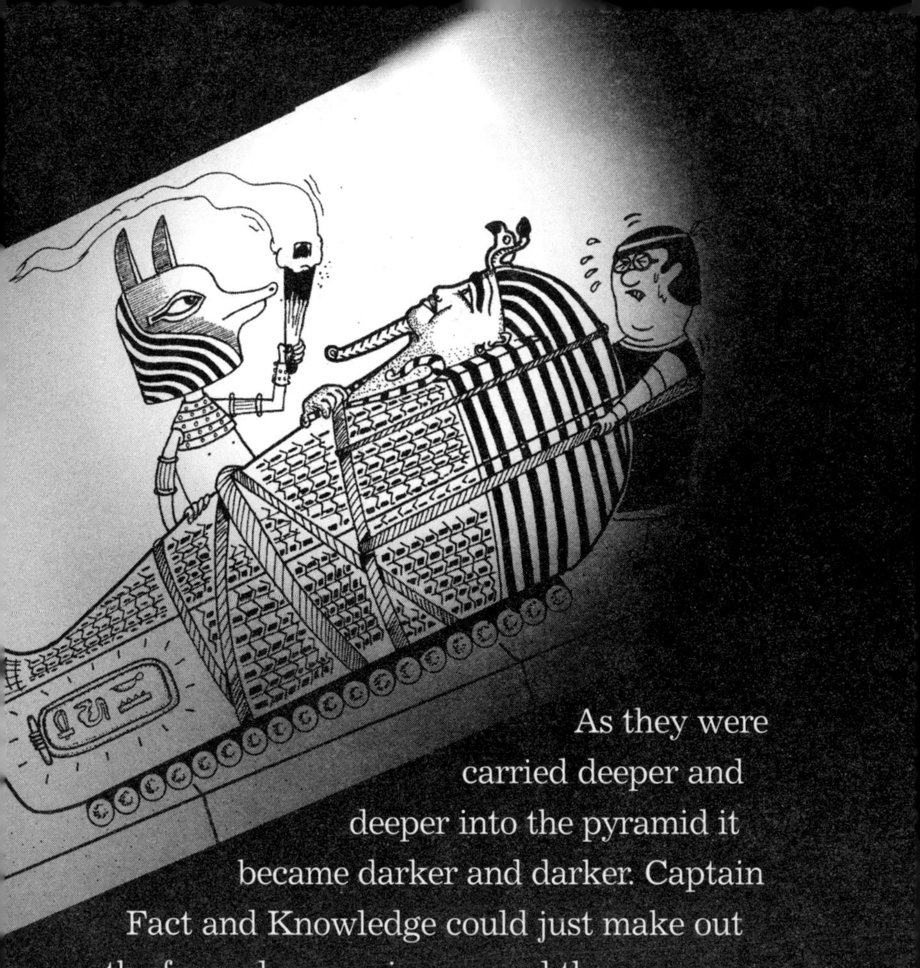

As they were carried deeper and deeper into the pyramid it became darker and darker. Captain Fact and Knowledge could just make out the funeral procession around them.

"What are all those funny pictures on the sarcophagus?" asked Knowledge.

"There's nothing funny about those pictures," said Captain Fact as his bandages began to jiggle, and he got ready for a . . .

FACT

ANCIENT EGYPTIAN WRITING IS CALLED HIEROGLYPHICS. INSTEAD OF LETTERS IT USES PICTURES, OR HIEROGLYPHS, OF WHICH THERE WERE MORE THAN 700!

FACT

HIEROGLYPHS REPRESENT DIFFERENT SOUNDS OR OBJECTS. THE SHAPES WERE BASED ON EVERYDAY THINGS FOUND IN ANCIENT EGYPT LIKE OWLS, DUCKS, AND WATER.

FACT

FOR CENTURIES NO ONE COULD UNDERSTAND HIEROGLYPHICS. BUT IN 1799 THE ROSETTA STONE WAS DISCOVERED. IT HAD A TEXT IN THREE LANGUAGES, ONE OF WHICH WAS ANCIENT GREEK AND ANOTHER, HIEROGLYPHICS—BY COMPARING THE TWO, THE CODE WAS CRACKED!

=water || =eye || =tr

ATTACK!!!

FACT

BECAUSE HIEROGLYPHICS WERE SO COMPLICATED, HARDLY ANYONE COULD READ OR WRITE. THIS MEANT THAT SCRIBES WERE HIGHLY PRIZED. LEARNING TO BE A SCRIBE TOOK FIVE YEARS OF TRAINING, AND YOU STARTED AT THE AGE OF NINE!

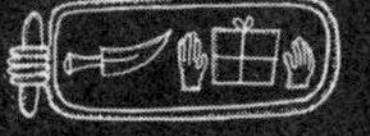

FACT

ANCIENT EGYPTIANS WROTE ON PAPYRUS, WHICH IS MADE FROM A REED THAT GROWS BY THE NILE. STRIPS OF THE REED WERE BEATEN AND WOVEN TO MAKE A KIND OF PAPER.

= snake | = star | = night | =

After being carried through increasingly narrow passages and ever steeper staircases, the funeral procession finally arrived in the secret burial chamber.

"I'm glad we finally got here," whispered Captain Fact. "That was the last of the dog biscuits."

Captain Fact and Knowledge, still in the mummy bandages, were carefully placed near the mummy and its hoard of possessions. The funeral party left, and there was a deep rumbling as a giant granite slab was slid across the entrance.

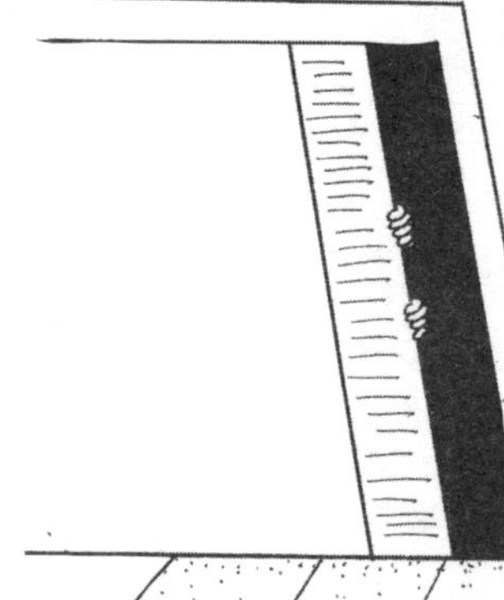

"Oh, no! We're sealed in," said Captain Fact. "That wasn't part of my plan."

He looked around. All around them were piles of offerings to the mummy.

"It looks like we got locked in a furniture shop," said Knowledge. "Look, there are beds, stools, cabinets, chairs . . ."

"There has to be something in here we can use to help us escape," said Captain Fact, rummaging through the treasures. But just then his feet began to itch, and he got ready for a . . .

FACT
FOR ALL YOUR
TOYS
YOU'LL NEVER GET BORED IN THE AFTERLIFE WITH A BOARD GAME TO ENTERTAIN YOU. NEW IN EBONY AND IVORY, ANCIENT EGYPT'S MOST POPULAR BOARD GAME: SENET.
MAKEUP
WHEN YOU MEET YOUR ANCESTORS IN THE AFTERLIFE, YOU'RE GOING TO WANT TO LOOK YOUR BEST. SO MAKE SURE YOU BRING YOUR MAKEUP BOXES AND MIRRORS.

AFTERLIFE NEEDS
SERVANTS
WHO WANTS TO WORK WHEN HE'S DEAD? NO ONE, SO TAKE SOME MODELS OF SERVANTS. THEY'LL COME TO LIFE WHEN YOU'RE DEAD AND DO ALL YOUR WORK FOR YOU! WHO COULD ASK FOR MORE?
MUSICAL INSTRUMENTS
FILL THE AFTERLIFE WITH SOUND USING ONE OF OUR WONDERFUL MUSICAL INSTRUMENTS. WE'VE GOT HARPS, FLUTES, AND RATTLES!
ATTACK!!!

After much rummaging around, Captain Fact emerged from the pile of goodies with a ceremonial spear.

"Grab an end of this spear, Knowledge, and pull," said Captain Fact. Without another word, the two of them set out to dislodge the granite slab.

CHAPTER 9
CURSE OF THE MUMMY!

It took a lot of pushing and panting, but Captain Fact and Knowledge finally moved the giant granite block. There was just enough room for them to squeeze through.

"What's that noise?" asked Captain Fact after he unbandaged his head. "It sounds like chewing!"

"It's nervous eating," pleaded Knowledge.

"Your nervous eating will actually help us," said Captain Fact. "You lead the way, and I'll log our coordinates into the Fact Watch. We'll relay the information to Professor Minuscule, and he can make a map to help save Sir Ramsbottom."

With Knowledge frantically munching dog biscuits and Captain Fact frantically tracking their course, the two superheroes undertook the death-defying task of exiting the pyramid in one piece. Everywhere there were traps and false entrances that could stop them.

"I think we're being followed," said Knowledge, between bites of his biscuit. "I hear footsteps."

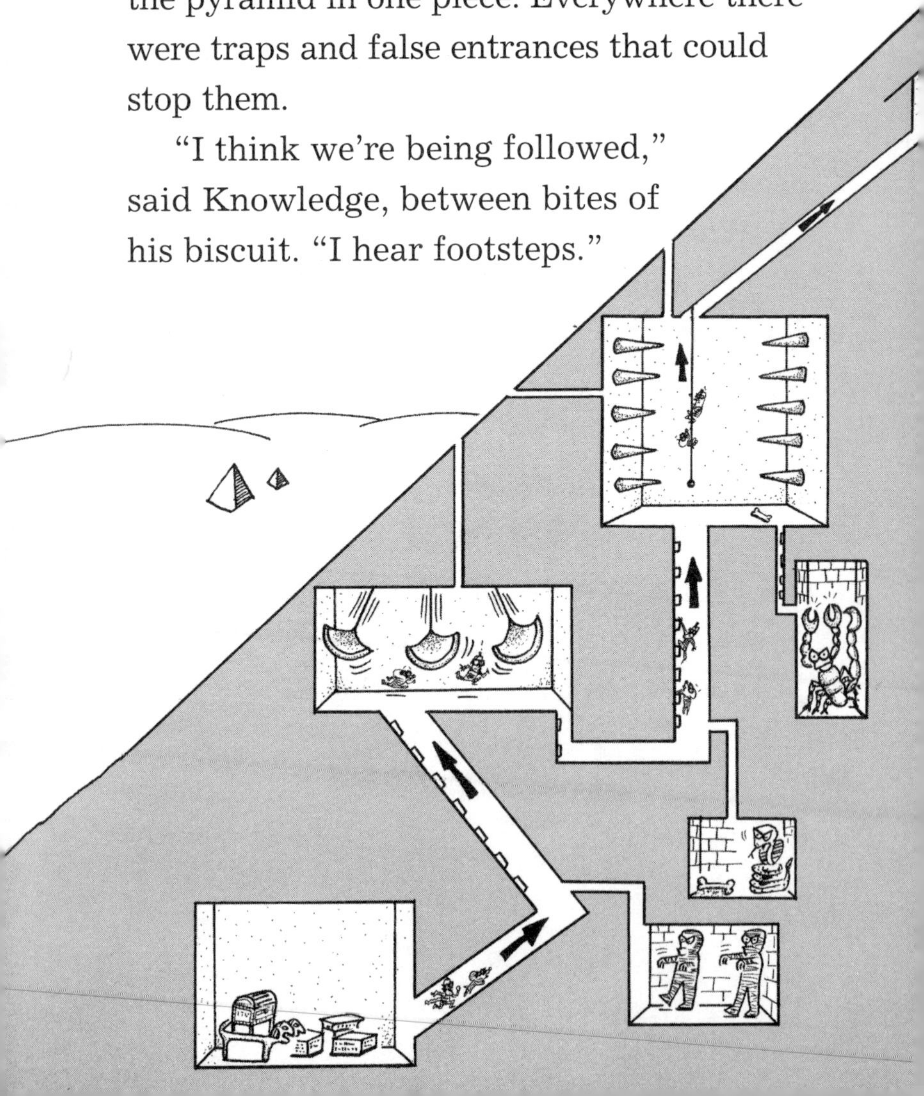

"I think you may be right. I thought I heard a door creak," said Captain Fact.

"I hope we haven't woken up the mummy," said Knowledge nervously.

"Factorella said something about the curse of the mummy, remember?" asked Captain Fact as his spine tingled and he felt the stirrings of another . . .

FACT
NOW SHOWING AT
REX CINEMA
MUMMY SEASON
TOMB With a View
"THEY WHO ENTER THIS SACRED TOMB SHALL BE VISITED BY THE WINGS OF DEATH!" NEWSPAPERS CLAIMED THAT THIS WAS WRITTEN OUTSIDE TUTANKHAMEN'S TOMB, BUT IN FACT THE REPORTERS HAD MADE IT UP!
MUMMY, I SHRANK THE KIDS
HOWARD CARTER WAS IN CHARGE OF THE EXPEDITION INSIDE TUTANKHAMEN'S TOMB. WHEN HE ENTERED THE TOMB, HIS PET CANARY WAS KILLED BY A COBRA. THE COBRA WAS THE SYMBOL OF THE PHARAOH! CREEPY!
ATTACK of the ALIEN MUMMIES
LORD CARNARVON, THE MAN WHO PAID FOR THE EXPEDITION TO FIND TUTANKHAMEN, DIED FOUR MONTHS AFTER HE ENTERED THE TOMB!

ATTACK!!!
Mummy and Hardy in
WAY OUT EAST
BUT . . . THERE COULD ACTUALLY BE A SCIENTIFIC EXPLANATION: "THE CURSE OF THE MUMMY" MIGHT BE THE RESULT OF TRAPPED BACTERIA OR ATOMIC RADIATION THAT WAS RELEASED WHEN THE TOMB WAS OPENED. NOT ONLY THAT, BUT MOST DEATHS RELATING TO THE TOMB CAN BE EXPLAINED RATIONALLY, AND HOWARD CARTER HIMSELF LIVED TO A RIPE OLD AGE!
MUMMY FROM THE BLACK LAGOON
LORD CARNARVON DIED FROM A MOSQUITO BITE THAT WENT SEPTIC. TUTANKHAMEN'S MUMMY HAD A SCAR ON HIS FACE IN EXACTLY THE SAME PLACE AS CARNARVON'S BITE!
TICKETS

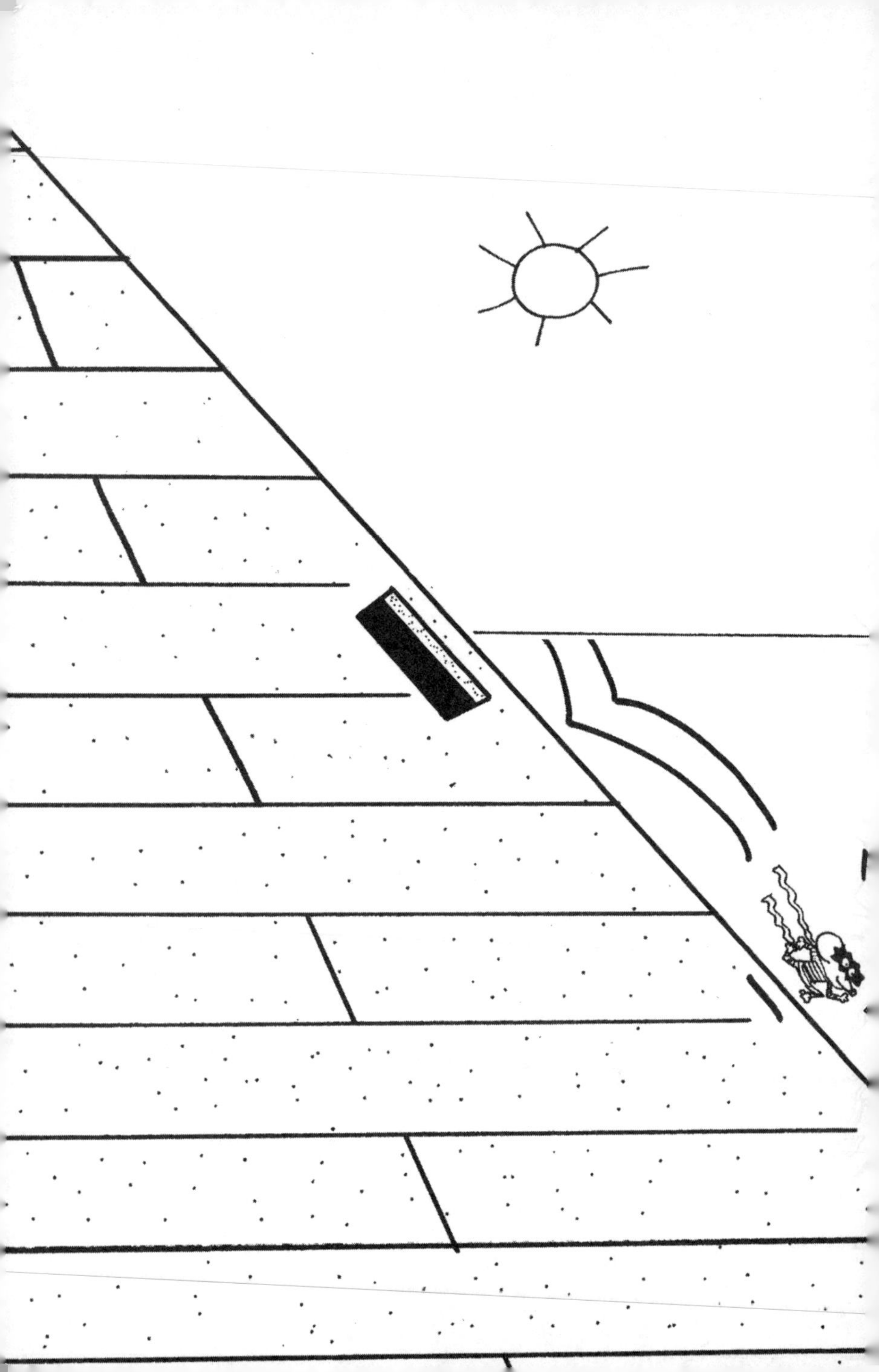

After what seemed like an eternity, Captain Fact and Knowledge finally saw daylight.

"We did it!" shouted Captain Fact as they stumbled into the bright sunlight. They were halfway up the side of the pyramid. "I feel amazing!"

"I feel stuffed," Knowledge said, groaning.

But Captain Fact wasn't listening. Turning, he dashed down the side of the pyramid. Knowledge followed. At the bottom, Captain Fact used the Fact Watch to make contact with Professor Minuscule.

"Come in, Professor Minuscule—do you read me?" he said.

"I hear you loud and clear, Captain Fact," crackled Professor Minuscule. "Congratulations! You've solved the mystery of the secret passage!"

"We couldn't have done it without Knowledge's dog biscuits," said Captain Fact, looking proudly at his furry friend.

"Well, those dog biscuits have saved the world's most famous archaeologist," said Professor Minuscule. "I've downloaded the coordinates you gave me, and as we speak, a map is being sent to the Egyptian authorities."

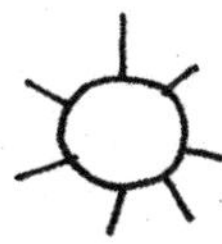

All of a sudden there was a loud noise and a doorway started to shimmer in the distance.

"The Time Portal should have arrived and be stabilizing," said Professor Minuscule. "I've set it so that you will return to your office in time for the evening weather forecast."

Captain Fact and Knowledge took a final look at the splendor of ancient Egypt before stepping through the Time Portal and back to modern times.

CHAPTER 10

AND NOW, THE WEATHER . . .

Unfortunately, the Time Portal was a little bit off. Rather than stepping out into their office, Captain Fact and Knowledge (in nonsuperhero form) emerged in the office gym, where the Boss was working out.

They barely got their masks off in time to run out the door.

As the Boss looked up from his exercise bike, he couldn't believe his eyes. "I could have sworn I just saw Thornhill and Puddles dressed up as mummies," gasped the Boss, rubbing his eyes, "I knew exercise wasn't good for you. I'm taking the rest of the day off!"

Cliff and Puddles sprinted to their office to get changed.

Having torn off their bandages, Cliff and Puddles dashed into the Makeup department.

"There you are, Cliff, I've been looking all over for you," said Lucy. "Captain Fact has done it again! He saved the day! Look, it's on the news now."

Cliff, Puddles, and Lucy glanced up at the TV monitor, which showed a recently rescued Sir Ramsbottom being interviewed.

"I think Sir Ramsbottom's dreamy," said Lucy, "but not as dreamy as Captain Fact. I'd like to be entombed in a pyramid with him!"

Cliff blushed as he and Puddles walked out of Makeup and stepped in front of the cameras.

And so, with Sir Ramsbottom safely back in his favorite museum, Cliff Thornhill and Puddles were back doing what they did worst—the weather.

Until the next crisis . . .

KNIFE & PACKER FACT!
KNIFE AND PACKER WOULD LOVE TO MEET A MUMMY AND PLAY THE WORLD'S SCARIEST-EVER GAME OF HIDE-AND-SEEK—IN A PYRAMID. YIKES!!!
7... 8... 9...
HiDE!